Rosie's Favourite Tales

EGMONT
We bring stories to life

First published in Great Britain 2012 by Egmont UK Limited
239 Kensington High Street, London W8 6SA

ISBN 978 1 4052 6316 0
51741/1
Printed in China

Contents

The Mystery of the Four Feathers

Rosie and Will were having a race.

Rosie was on her Twooter, pushing it as fast as it would go. Will was on his Go Speeder.

"Turbo blasters to max power!" yelled Will as he tried to zoom ahead.

But Rosie and Will were neck and neck as they sped towards the finish line.

Raggles was standing next to the finish line. He was watching the race carefully. It was his job to decide who was the winner.

Suddenly, Raggles was hit by a flurry of feathers! It was Bluebird. She had accidentally flown into him. Raggles and Bluebird fell to the ground, all tumbled up and in a muddle.

Bluebird quickly dusted herself off and flew on. Raggles jumped up too, but the race was over and he hadn't seen who had won!

"**Y**ee-hah! I'm the champ!" cheered Will.

"No, I won," said Rosie, crossly. "Didn't I, Raggles?"

Poor Raggles looked worried. "Um, I'm not really sure," he explained.

Rosie was disappointed. "But I won," she insisted.

Raggles didn't like to see Rosie upset. "Let's go home and make some cookies," he suggested. "That'll be more fun."

Back at the Playhouse, Rosie and Raggles mixed together the ingredients for their cookies.

"I still can't believe you missed me winning the race," grumbled Rosie.

As Raggles looked up to reply, he noticed something odd about Rosie. The button that she always wore in her hair was missing.

Rosie was very upset when Raggles told her. She rushed to the mirror to see for herself.

"We have to find it," she said. "It must have fallen off during the race."

And they set off to look for it at once.

Meanwhile, Holly was knocking on Big Bear's door. When he didn't reply, she carefully pushed the door open. Even though it was late in the day, Big Bear was still curled up in bed, snoring!

"Wake up!" said Holly, shaking Big Bear. "Teddy has gone missing."

"Huh?" said Big Bear, startled.

He looked for his alarm clock to check the time, but that was missing too! In its place was a brightly coloured little parcel.

"That's funny," said Holly. "I found a little parcel in place of Teddy, too!"

Rosie and Raggles were busy searching for the missing button. They looked all along the track where the race had been. Just as they reached the end, Raggles noticed something.

"What's this?" he asked, picking up a colourful little parcel.

"Never mind that," said Rosie. "We must find my button. I was at Big Bear's house this morning, let's go and look there."

Rosie and Raggles walked over to Big Bear's house. Big Bear and Holly were sitting outside, looking at their parcels.

The friends quickly told each other about their missing things and the mysterious packages they had found in their place.

"Holly's teddy, Big Bear's clock, my button … perhaps someone is taking our special things!" gasped Rosie.

"Well, this calls for a serious investigation," said Raggles.

Rosie and Raggles didn't know where to start the investigation, so they set off to see Saffie. She was wise and might be able to help.

Saffie listened to their news. She pondered the problem, then sighed mysteriously: "Can a dry desert find rain ... or does rain find the desert?"

"So, instead of looking for the culprit, we should let the culprit come to us," said Rosie, happily. Now she knew what to do!

Rosie's plan was to lay a trap. But she needed something special to use as bait.

Just then, Will whizzed past in his Go Speeder. "Ready for a rematch?" he called.

"Not just yet," said Rosie, having an idea. "Please can I borrow your football?"

Will didn't mind lending his football. But it was his favourite ball, so he asked Rosie to take good care of it.

Rosie and Raggles put Will's ball in the middle of the playground. Then they hid in the bushes to watch. If someone tried to take the ball, they would catch them.

They hadn't been there long when there was rustling in the bushes, but it was only Big Bear and Holly coming to find them.

Rosie explained about the trap.

"But I can't see a football," said Holly.

It was true! While they had been talking, Will's ball had gone! All that remained was a small, brightly wrapped parcel.

The friends set out to find Will, and found him chatting to Oakley. He was very upset when Rosie told him about his ball.

Rosie explained how everyone had lost something special, so she had tried to lay a trap. She was very sorry that it had gone wrong.

"And all that's left are these little parcels?" asked Will.

"Maybe we should open them," said Holly.

Everyone nodded and ripped open the shiny paper. Inside were brightly-coloured feathers!

Everyone stared at the feathers. What could they mean?

Suddenly there was a loud ringing noise, **ring-a-ling, ring-a-ling!**

"Is that me?" said Oakley in surprise. The noise was coming from amongst his leaves.

"It sounds like my alarm clock!" said Big Bear.

Oakley shook his branches ... and out fell Bluebird with a **crash!** She was still sitting in her nest and scattered around her was Big Bear's alarm clock, Holly's teddy, Rosie's button and Will's football!

"**B**luebird," said Rosie, "why did you take all of these things?"

Bluebird hung her head in shame.

"I saw everyone with their special things," said Bluebird, "and I wanted something special too! So I did a swap. I left you all a feather."

"But you shouldn't borrow things without asking," said Big Bear.

"I know," sobbed Bluebird. "And it turned out that the only really special things for me were my feathers. I've really missed them."

"**E**veryone misses their special things," said Rosie, kindly. "That's why they're special."

The friends swapped so they all had their favourite things back again. Bluebird waved her feathers with glee and promised never to borrow something without asking again.

"Raggles," said Rosie, looking concerned. "Don't you have a special thing?"

"Oh yes," said Raggles, smiling. "Sometimes it's my dinosaur, then there's my squeezy parrot, oh and today there are my cookies!" And he rushed back to the Playhouse to finish baking them!

Raggles the Reporter

Rosie was oiling the wheels of her Twooter. Raggles was watching her. He was holding a little notepad and a pencil.

"Um. Do you like your Twooter, Rosie?" Raggles asked.

"Of course I do!" laughed Rosie.

Raggles scribbled Rosie's answer in his notepad and then smiled proudly.

"Today I'm Raggles the Reporter!" he announced. "And I'm writing my very own newspaper."

"**H**ow's this for my first story?" continued Raggles, "Rosie oils Twooter ... And it's faster than ever!"

"Well, it's very nice," said Rosie, kindly, "but it's not very exciting."

Raggles nodded. Rosie was right, he needed better stories for his newspaper to be a success.

"Just follow your nose," Rosie advised. "You'll soon find a story everyone wants to read!"

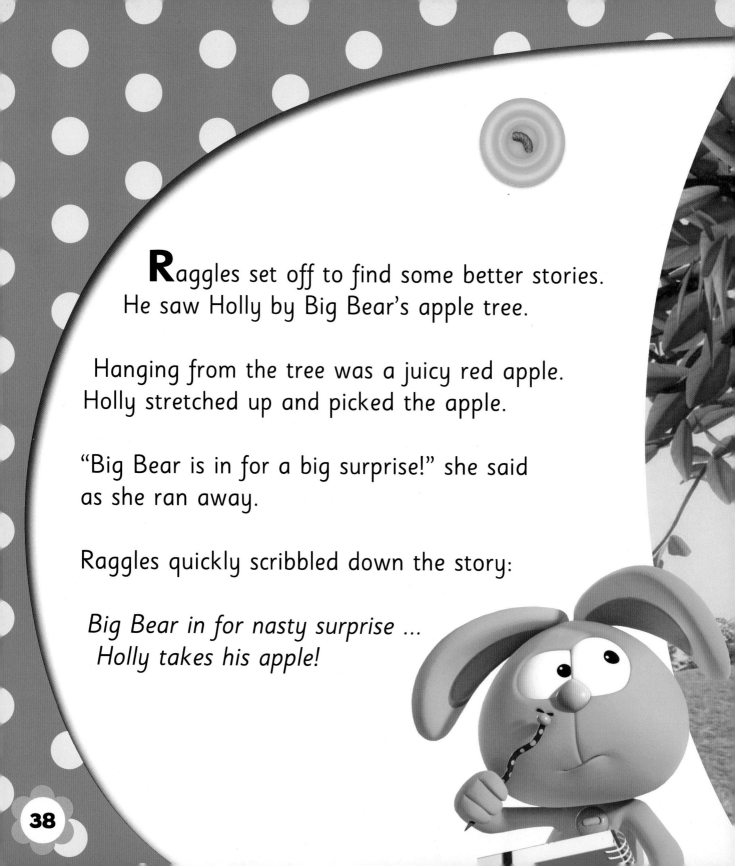

Raggles set off to find some better stories. He saw Holly by Big Bear's apple tree.

Hanging from the tree was a juicy red apple. Holly stretched up and picked the apple.

"Big Bear is in for a big surprise!" she said as she ran away.

Raggles quickly scribbled down the story:

*Big Bear in for nasty surprise ...
Holly takes his apple!*

Meanwhile, Bluebird was practising her magic. She was using a special spell to move her nest into a new tree, but the magic wasn't working!

"Come on, nest," squawked Bluebird, crossly. "Get up there, into that tree."

But the nest didn't move.

"Unhelpful nest," Bluebird muttered, "and this tree is silly!"

She stomped away in a huff.

Raggles was watching from behind a bush.

"Bluebird says trees are silly," repeated Raggles, "Now that's a brilliant story!

Raggles scribbled the story into his notepad and smiled.

"Rosie was right," he thought. "I just have to follow my nose and I find amazing stories."

He set off to find his next big scoop.

At the bottom of Oakley's Hill, Raggles saw Will.

Will had a football. He placed the ball carefully on the ground. He then took a big run-up and kicked the ball up the hill. It bashed Oakley on the nose!

"Ouch!" cried Oakley.

"Ha, ha!" yelled Will as he ran away from the hill. "Nice one!"

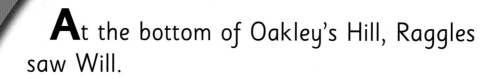

Raggles scribbled down another story: *Will kicks ball at Oakley ... then runs away laughing!*

He shut his notepad. He had enough stories for a whole newspaper now! He hurried away to write it.

Just then, Will came running back. He'd been to fetch the ball.

"Great save, Oakley!" he shouted.

"Thank you," chuckled Oakley, cheerfully.

They were playing football together!

Raggles was running to the Playhouse to write his newspaper when he bumped into Rosie.

"Did you get any good stories?" Rosie asked.

"A whole newspaper's worth!" replied Raggles, smiling happily.

Rosie wanted to read the stories straight away, but Raggles said she would have to wait until the newspaper was written.

"It'll be a surprise!" said Raggles.

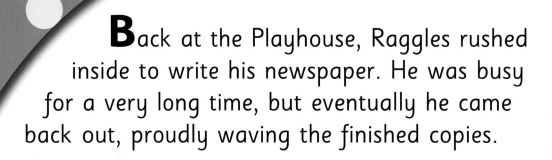

Back at the Playhouse, Raggles rushed inside to write his newspaper. He was busy for a very long time, but eventually he came back out, proudly waving the finished copies.

Rosie and Raggles jumped onto the Twooter and went to deliver the newspapers. Raggles threw a copy to everyone they passed.

Soon, everyone was reading the news!

While Oakley was reading the newspaper, Rosie and Raggles rested in the shade of his branches.

Oakley frowned as he read. "Bluebird says trees are silly," he said. "What a cheek!"

"But Bluebird loves trees," said Rosie, surprised.

Rosie borrowed the newspaper from Oakley and quickly looked through the pages.

"Oh, Raggles!" she said. "What have you done?"

Before Raggles could answer, Bluebird arrived. She was very cross.

"I didn't say all trees were silly!" huffed Bluebird. "Just one tree."

Raggles looked confused.

Then Big Bear and Holly walked up. "Holly picked that apple as a surprise for me!" said Big Bear, in a hurt voice.

"And I was only playing football with Oakley," added Will, coming to join them. "He was in goal!"

Raggles looked down at the ground.

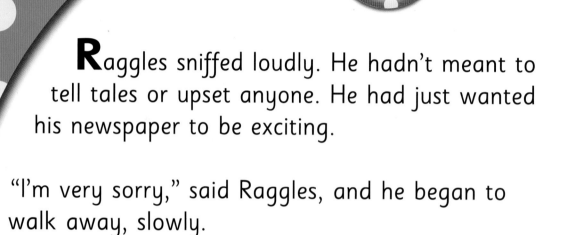

Raggles sniffed loudly. He hadn't meant to tell tales or upset anyone. He had just wanted his newspaper to be exciting.

"I'm very sorry," said Raggles, and he began to walk away, slowly.

Rosie could see Raggles was sorry for all the trouble he had caused. She followed him and put an arm around his shoulder.

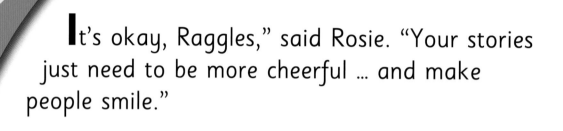

It's okay, Raggles," said Rosie. "Your stories just need to be more cheerful ... and make people smile."

"A newspaper that makes people laugh?" wondered Raggles. "Now that's a brilliant idea!"

"Come on, then!" said Rosie. "I'll show you."

Rosie helped Raggles to write a brand new newspaper. And this time, it was full of fun!

The friends sat on Oakley's Hill, reading Raggles' new newspaper.

"Here's a picture of me!" pointed out Big Bear, excitedly.

"And here's a good joke," cried Will. "What did the pirate say when he dropped an anchor on his foot?"

"Ooh arrrrrr!" laughed Bluebird.

"It's the best newspaper ever," said Oakley. "Well done, Raggles."

Raggles beamed. He caught Rosie's eye and she smiled too.

That night, as they snuggled up in their beds, Raggles and Rosie talked about how nice it was to make their friends laugh.

"And I've got a new joke," giggled Rosie. "What do you read when you want to go to sleep ... a snoozepaper!"

Raggles chuckled, and then he yawned. It had been fun being Reporter Raggles for the day!

As he dropped off to sleep Raggles thought, "I wonder what I'll be tomorrow?"

The Special Invitation

Rosie and Raggles had spent all morning playing with the dressing-up box, but now it was time to tidy up.

"I think that's everything, Raggles," said Rosie, dropping the final shoe into the box.

"Oh good," said Raggles, and he let out a large yawn. "Now for some serious hammock time!"

But just as Raggles bounced into his hammock for a rest, there was a rat-a-tat-tat at the door. Rosie and Raggles had a visitor!

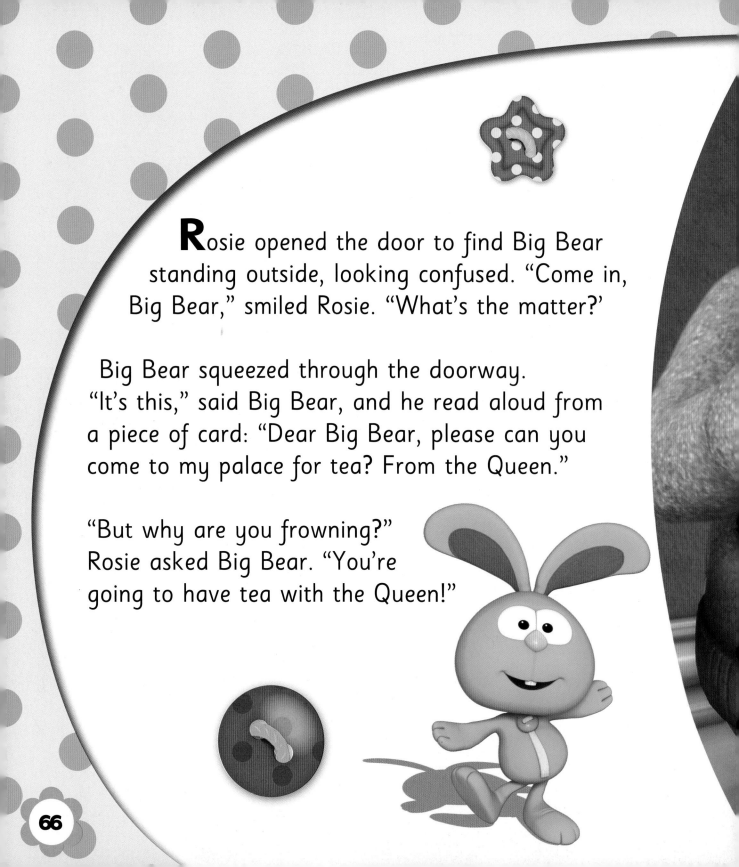

Rosie opened the door to find Big Bear standing outside, looking confused. "Come in, Big Bear," smiled Rosie. "What's the matter?'

Big Bear squeezed through the doorway. "It's this," said Big Bear, and he read aloud from a piece of card: "Dear Big Bear, please can you come to my palace for tea? From the Queen."

"But why are you frowning?" Rosie asked Big Bear. "You're going to have tea with the Queen!"

"**I**'m worried," Big Bear sighed.
"I've never had tea with the Queen before!
What if I get crumbs on my whiskers?
Or jelly on my paws?"

"Well, luckily you've come to the right place,"
giggled Rosie. "Raggles
and I will teach you
how to have tea with
a queen."

A grin spread across Big Bear's
face. "Oh, thank you both!"
he beamed.

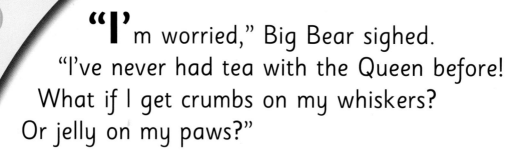

69

"**F**irst," Rosie told Big Bear kindly, "you have to dress right."

They all looked through the dressing-up box, and pulled out a pink cape, an orange top hat and a pair of purple ear-warmers. Big Bear tried each of them on, but he didn't like any of them.

Rosie thought for a moment, then she had an idea. "Wait there!" she called as she dashed away. She came back holding a small red bow tie and gently put it on Big Bear.

"Perfect!" said Raggles.

"Next," said Raggles, "you have to walk tall, with confidence!"

"Easy peasy," said Big Bear and he did his best walk. But he still walked like a bear.

"We'll get you walking like a prince," said Rosie. She gently placed a book on top of his head to help him stand up straight. "Now try to walk up Oakley's Hill."

And off Big Bear went, trying as hard as he could not to drop the book. He felt very silly, but Raggles cheered him on.

At the same time, Will was hiding in a flower bed, watching as Big Bear struggled to balance the book on his head.

"This is my best trick ever! Big Bear having tea with the Queen," he snorted. "As if!"

As he watched Big Bear, Will's eyes fell on Holly, who was in the playground.

"I wonder if Holly would like to go to tea with the Queen too?" Will sniggered to himself. He took a postcard and a pencil out of his pocket and began to write another invitation.

Up on Oakley's Hill, Rosie, Raggles and Big Bear were practising drinking tea.

"Great slurping!" said Raggles as Big Bear took a really long slurp of his tea.

Big Bear felt very proud of his slurping skills. But there was one last lesson to learn – how to speak clearly.

"Repeat clearly after me," Oakley smiled. "Rosie and Raggles ran around the roundabout." Every word was spoken perfectly! Big Bear took a big breath ...

"Rosie and Raggles round-a-ran about the run ... oh." He stopped. Rosie and Raggles smiled at him kindly.

Big Bear tried again. "Rosie and roundabout raggled round and ran and about ..." He'd got muddled again!

But Big Bear was determined. He let out a big sigh, took in a big breath and tried one last time. "Rosie and Raggles ran around the roundabout."

He'd done it! He was ready to meet the Queen.

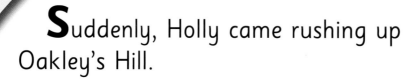

Suddenly, Holly came rushing up Oakley's Hill.

"I've got an invitation!" Holly told them, waving a piece of card in front of her. "It says, 'Dear Holly, please can you come to my palace for tea? From the Queen.'"

Rosie was speechless, but suddenly, there was more commotion as Bluebird fell out of Oakley's branches!

"I, Bluebird, have been invited to tea with the Queen!" she announced grandly.

"**N**ot you as well!" said Raggles, as Rosie gently took Bluebird's invitation from under her wing. It was exactly the same as Big Bear's and Holly's!

"I know this handwriting!" said Rosie.

"I didn't know you knew the Queen, Rosie," said Oakley in a shocked voice.

"I don't," Rosie said. "But I do know who wrote all these invitations. It was Will!"

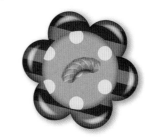

Everyone was very upset.

"But I've had a wash!" cried Big Bear.

"And I've polished my beak!" complained Bluebird grumpily.

Holly said nothing, but her eyes filled with tears. She had been so excited about meeting the Queen, and it was all just a trick.

As Rosie looked at her disappointed friends, an idea popped into her head. "Follow me, everyone!" she smiled. "We're going to have tea with the Queen after all."

Meanwhile, Will was still watching his friends, laughing harder than ever. They had all fallen for his trick! But when they all began to walk towards the Playhouse, Will was puzzled. What was going on? He ran ahead of them and sat down on a swing.

"Where are you going?" he asked Big Bear, Holly and Bluebird as they walked past.

"To have tea with the Queen," Holly replied.

"What?" Will said. "It was just a joke!"

"I can assure you there is nothing funny about tea with Her Majesty," said Bluebird in a posh voice.

"Well, can I come too?" Will asked.

"Have you got an invitation?" Big Bear said.

"No," Will told him.

"Sorry!" came Bluebird's reply, but she didn't sound very sorry at all. As they all walked away towards the Playhouse, Will felt very left out. Maybe his trick wasn't so funny after all, now his friends were having tea without him.

Back at the Playhouse, Her Royal Highness Rosie and her loyal knight Sir Raggles welcomed their guests to their palace. Rosie wore a shiny crown, and the table was full of cakes and jelly.

Will peered in the window, and decided to ask if he could join in. He knocked on the Playhouse door, and Raggles answered.

"Hello, Raggles," said Will quietly. "Can I have tea with you all too?"

"You may," replied Raggles. "But you'll have to be our waiter to make up for tricking Big Bear, Bluebird and Holly."

Will thought for a moment. "OK," he sighed, and soon he was wearing Rosie's best black jacket and carrying a tray.

Rosie, Raggles, Big Bear, Bluebird and Holly sat around the table and admired how well Big Bear had remembered everything he'd learnt — he sat up straight, slurped his tea and looked very smart in his bow tie. It was just like having tea with the real Queen!

"Except," smiled Rosie, "in this palace you can get jelly on your paws!"

And everyone laughed — even Will!

Super Will

Raggles loves to fly his kite. In fact, sometimes he's so busy flying his kite that he doesn't look where he is going, which was exactly what happened one day. Now his kite was stuck in a tree.

"We're going to need the kite grabbers, Raggles," said Rosie.

Raggles handed her a pair of purple grabbers. Soon Rosie had rescued Raggles' kite, but it had a big rip in it. Raggles was very sad.

95

Then Rosie and Raggles heard a wail coming from the bridge.

"What's that?" gasped Raggles.

"Sounds like someone's in trouble," Rosie replied. "Lets go and see if we can help."

Together they ran down to the bridge, where they found Holly crying because her Teddy had accidentally fallen onto a rock in the middle of the stream.

"If only we had something to grab Teddy with," Rosie thought aloud. She didn't like seeing Holly so upset.

Rosie looked over at Raggles, who was still holding the kite grabbers. They were just what she needed!

Rosie used the grabbers to reach Teddy and soon he was safe and sound in Holly's arms.

Just then, Will came whizzing up on his Go Speeder. "Is everything all right Holly?" he said, worried. "I heard you crying."

But Holly wasn't listening. She was too busy gazing at Rosie and Raggles. "My heroes!" she sighed happily as she hugged her teddy.

After Big Bear told him what had happened, Will couldn't believe it. Rosie and Raggles weren't his idea of heroes. They weren't even wearing superhero clothes!

Later that day, Will came out from his house wearing a cape and an eye-mask. He strode up to Saffie.

"Ta-da!" he said. "What do you think?"

Saffie looked confused. "Will, why are you wearing an eye mask?" she asked.

"I'm not Will anymore, I'm Super Will," he declared. "Now I just need someone to rescue so I can prove to everyone that I'm the real superhero around here, not Rosie or Raggles."

With that, Will jumped on his Go Speeder and sped off.

First, Super Will went to see Oakley, but he didn't need rescuing. Then Will spotted Holly's teddy all alone behind a tree. "Holly must have lost it," Will said to himself.

He picked up the teddy and dashed off to find Holly. She was sat with her head in her hands, and when she looked up, she was very surprised to see Will standing in front of her.

"Here, I've saved your teddy," he said proudly.

"But he didn't need saving," she smiled. "He's playing hide and seek with Big Bear, Little Bear and me!"

103

Next, Will went to the Playhouse, where Rosie and Raggles were sitting outside. Will remembered Raggles' torn kite, and wondered if perhaps he could mend it for him, but Rosie had beaten him to it.

"Oh," Will sighed. "No one needs my help after all."

"You could help me fly my kite again," said Raggles.

That gave Will an idea. Perhaps if Raggles got his kite stuck again, then Will could rescue it for him this time.

"But there's no wind," Rosie told them both. "And there are too many trees around here."

"I know how to make your kite fly, Raggles," Will cried. "Follow me!"

Will led Raggles over to the Go Speeder and told him to sit in the front seat. Will got in next to him and they set off. As the Go Speeder sped forwards, the wind from the movement blew the kite into the air. It was flying again!

"Remember Will, don't go too near the trees," Raggles told him. But Will had other ideas. He kept pushing the Go Speeder closer and closer to the trees, and before they knew it, the kite was stuck again!

Will was very pleased that he could now rescue the kite. Raggles wanted to get Rosie, but Will was determined to show what a hero he was!

"You don't need Rosie, you've got Super Will!" said Will as he clambered up the tree.

"But the kite is ripping!" shouted Raggles. "Stop, Will!"

Raggles ran back to the Playhouse to fetch Rosie and the kite grabbers, but it was too late. By the time he came back, the kite was already torn. Will had tugged it out of the tree in his rush to be a hero. Raggles was heartbroken.

109

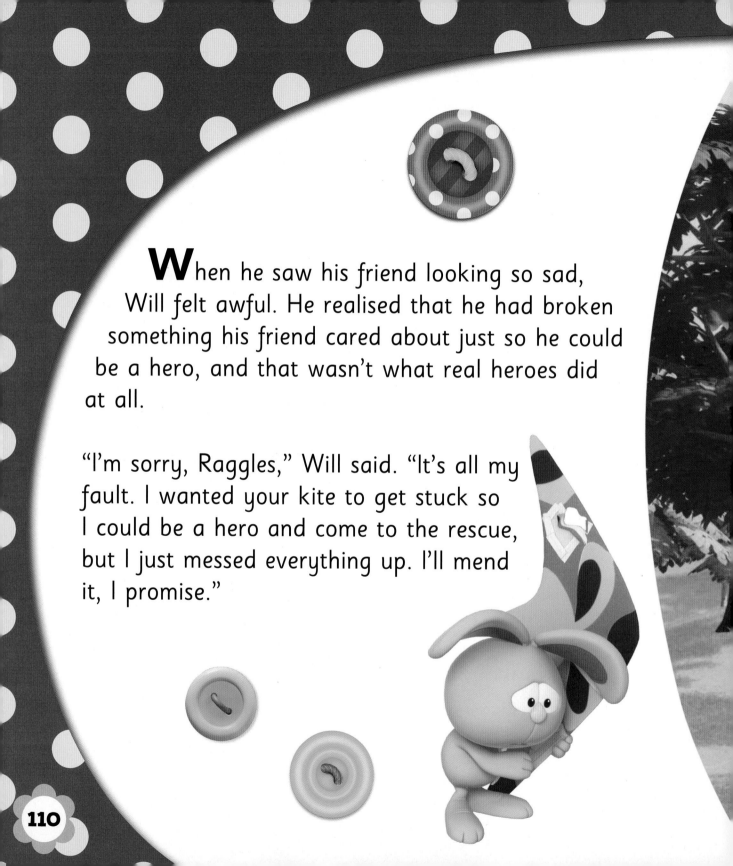

When he saw his friend looking so sad, Will felt awful. He realised that he had broken something his friend cared about just so he could be a hero, and that wasn't what real heroes did at all.

"I'm sorry, Raggles," Will said. "It's all my fault. I wanted your kite to get stuck so I could be a hero and come to the rescue, but I just messed everything up. I'll mend it, I promise."

Raggles didn't have a chance to reply, because at that moment, Big Bear and Holly raced up to them.

"Have you seen Little Bear?" Big Bear asked in a panic. "We were playing hide and seek, but we can't find him anywhere!"

Everyone forgot about the kite. This was a real emergency!

"OK," said Will. "We'll all look together. Rosie and Raggles, you look in the swing pods. Big Bear and Holly, go and ask Saffie if she has seen him. I'll look in the playground."

Will searched high and low in the playground for Little Bear, but there was no sign of him. Then something strange caught his eye. The flags in the maze were changing!

"Someone is in the maze," Will said to himself. "Perhaps it's Little Bear?"

Will jumped into his Go Speeder and rushed over to the maze.

"Little Bear!" he shouted, as he sped into the maze. "Little Bear, is that you?"

In the middle of the maze, Little Bear was feeling very sorry for himself, as he changed the flags one more time. He was sure that no one would ever find him and he would never find his way out. Just then, he heard a voice calling his name!

"I'm here!" Little Bear shouted.

Will raced around the maze, and eventually he reached the middle. Little Bear ran over to Will and gave him the biggest hug he had ever given anyone.

"My hero!" Little Bear giggled, and Will glowed with pride.

"Come on, let's get you home," Will said, taking Little Bear's hand. "Big Bear is very worried about you!"

Big Bear was overjoyed to have
Little Bear home again, safe and sound.
Everyone was impressed with Will for
noticing the changing flags and for thinking
that it might be Little Bear moving them.

"That was very clever!" said Raggles.

"Maybe we should all call you Super Will after all,"
beamed Rosie.

"I think I prefer just being Will," said Will with a
shy smile. "But I have one more superhero thing to
do." And with that he took off his cape and handed
it to Raggles.

"What's this for?" Raggles asked.

"You'll see," said Will.

119

That evening, Rosie and Raggles sat outside the playhouse watching Raggles' new kite flying in the breeze. Raggles carefully pulled it back in and looked at it admiringly.

"Super Will had a super idea, didn't he, Raggles?" said Rosie.

"He certainly did, Rosie," Raggles giggled, holding up his new kite. "And now, thanks to his cape, I have a super kite too!"

The Call of the Wild

One day, up on Oakley's Hill, Rosie and her friends were playing a guessing game.

"Guess what I am," said Big Bear. He dropped to his knees and let out a tiny squeaking noise. **Squeak! Squeak! Squeak!**

"A rusty wheel?' guessed Raggles.

"Someone crying?" asked Holly

Bluebird, who was sat in Oakley's branches staring at other birds flying in the sky, sighed loudly.

"Big Bear's a mouse," she said sadly.

"**W**ell done, Bluebird!" Big Bear beamed. "Now it's your turn!"

Bluebird opened her beak and let out the same loud noise as the birds in the sky.
CAW! CAW! CAW!

"Well, that's easy," said Raggles. "You're a bird!"

"I'm a migrating bird, actually," Bluebird told him. She looked sadly at the birds in the sky again.

"What is *migrating?*" asked Holly.

"It's when we fly to faraway places," Bluebird answered. "It's like a long, tropical holiday where we can paddle in the sea, play in the sand and eat fancy fruits."

A bird fluttered down from the flock in the sky. It was Teal. Bluebird flew off to greet her, and together they settled on top of the fountain.

"You have to migrate," Teal told Bluebird. "We're birds. It's what we do!"

"I know, "said Bluebird, "but what about my friends? I can't leave them."

"They'll understand," Teal told her. "Just think of all the fun you'll be missing if you don't come."

Bluebird didn't know what to do. She needed time to think.

Back at Oakley's Hill, Rosie was worried.

"I think Bluebird might be planning to migrate," she said.

"She can't leave us!" cried Will.

"Who will wake me up in the morning if she goes?" wondered Big Bear.

"And what will happen to her magic if she goes away and forgets to practise?" said Holly.

They all agreed that they had to do something. If it was a tropical holiday Bluebird wanted, then that's what they'd give her!

Rosie and her friends spent the rest of the afternoon creating a tropical paradise.

Big Bear and Holly made the playground look like a beach. They made palm trees out of cardboard, put out deckchairs and even hung a hammock for Bluebird to relax in!

Meanwhile, Rosie and Raggles made fruit smoothies and Will put some wings on his Go Speeder so it looked like an aeroplane. After all, Bluebird deserved to travel in style!

Soon, everything was ready. "Time for Operation Exotic Holiday!" beamed Rosie.

They found Bluebird perched on the Pod Swing, looking very sorry for herself.

"There you are, Bluebird," called Rosie. "It's a good job we found you!"

"You almost missed your flight!" said Will.

Bluebird looked confused. "Do you mean my flight with the rest of the birds?" she asked.

"No," Rosie giggled as she revealed Will's Go Speeder. "Today you'll be flying on Will Airways!"

Will had attached the Go Pod to the back of his Go Speeder. Inside he had made a special seat for Bluebird.

"Oooh," said Bluebird excitedly, as she climbed aboard. "Where are we going?"

"Somewhere very special," Will told her. "Now please fasten your seatbelt and get ready for take-off!"

Will made the noise of a jet engine and they sped off. In fact, they sped off a little faster than Bluebird would have liked, as back in the Go Pod, she was bouncing all over the place!

When they arrived at the Playground, Bluebird couldn't hide her disappointment.

"The Playground?" she squawked. "This isn't special – I come here every day!"

"Not like this, you don't," laughed Rosie, and with that, Bluebird saw Holly's palm trees, the deckchairs in the sandpit and the hammock. She was amazed!

"Welcome to Bluebird Beach!" cheered Rosie, Will and Raggles.

"Wow, it's the best beach ever!" said Bluebird.

Rosie was thrilled that Bluebird liked the beach. But her happiness didn't last very long!

First, Bluebird got stuck in a deckchair after it broke when she sat down.

Then Raggles tripped when he was bringing Bluebird's fruit smoothie. The smoothie splashed all over Bluebird, soaking her feathers!

After Rosie cleaned her up, Big Bear suggested that Bluebird tried a relaxing swing in the hammock. But Big Bear swung the hammock so hard that Bluebird was thrown out of it and on to the trampoline. It wasn't very relaxing at all!

139

So far, the plan for Bluebird Beach had been a disaster! But Rosie wasn't going to give up.

"There's still lots more holiday excitement!" Rosie told Bluebird. She sounded much cheerier than she felt.

"Is there?" Bluebird asked nervously. She'd had about as much holiday excitement as she could take!

Just as Rosie started to reply, Will interrupted her. "Ladies and Gentlemen, if I could ask you to return to the aeroplane we will soon be continuing on our journey."

Bluebird hesitated for a moment, then she got back in the Go Pod for another bumpy ride.

They arrived at Oakley's Hill, where they found Oakley draped in tropical fruit. Rosie, who had ridden her Twooter alongside the Go Speeder, was being a tour guide.

"Here's a tree covered in tasty ..." she said

"Ahem, Rosie," Oakley interrupted, looking worried.

'... exotic treats for us to eat," she continued.

"ROSIE!" Will shouted, pointing to the Go Speeder. He'd forgotten to put the brakes on, and now it was rolling back down the hill, with Bluebird inside!

The Go Speeder came to a stop just near the bridge.

Rosie and Will ran down to help Bluebird. When they released her seatbelt, she stood up and shook herself.

"Well, that was … fast," Bluebird gasped.

Rosie, Will and Bluebird heard a bird calling above them. It was Teal.

"Come on, Bluebird!" she called. "It's time to go."

Bluebird climbed out of the Go Pod and, without saying a word, she flew into the air.

"Oh," Rosie sighed. "She's leaving us."

Later that day, the friends gathered on Oakley's Hill. They were all very upset that Bluebird had gone. Suddenly, they heard a voice.

"Coooooeeeee! It's only me!" it said. It was Bluebird!

"We thought you'd migrated," said Big Bear in disbelief.

"Are you kidding?" beamed Bluebird. "The effort you all put in made me realise that there's nowhere else I'd rather be. In fact, it's so much fun here, I've invited some of the other birds to stay, too!"

Not only had Bluebird stayed, but now there were new friends to play with too, which made everyone very happy indeed.

As they walked back to the Playhouse, Rosie and Raggles talked about where they would like to migrate.

"I'd like to go somewhere that's lots of fun," said Raggles. "Oh, and there'd have to be lots of food to eat ..."

"Well, you do get very peckish, Raggles," smiled Rosie.

"I know where I'd migrate!" Raggles said with a big smile. "To the Playhouse for tea!"